W9-AVJ-863

Down and Out In

Purgatory

Down and Out In

Purgatory

Tim Powers

SUBTERRANEAN PRESS 2016

First Edition

ISBN
978-1-59606-781-3

Subterranean Press
PO Box 190106
Burton, MI 48519

subterraneanpress.com

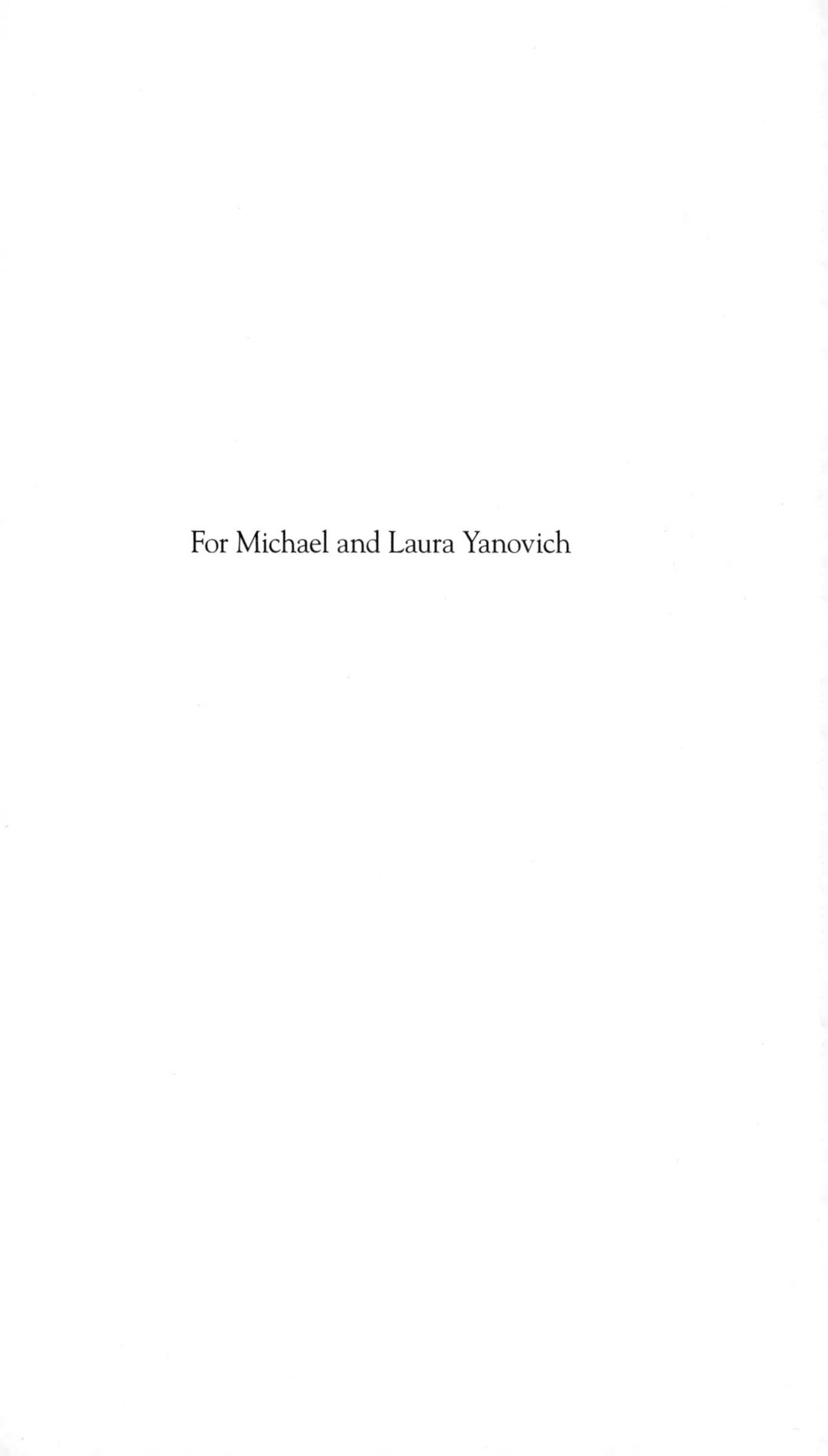

For Michael and Laura Yanovich

"I've always thought that death puts an end to the possibilities of revenge."

—PETER O'DONNELL

Before you embark on a journey of revenge, dig two graves.

—CONFUCIUS

1

"This way. Keep the clipboard visible and don't meet anybody's eye. Look like you work here, right?"

The young man in the white lab coat led the way down the fluorescent-lit hallway, past several tall stacks of cardboard boxes labeled *Can Liners,* and Holbrook momentarily wondered if they were very big can liners. The cool air smelled only of Lysol and the young man's after shave. Holbrook had to step ahead and look at the man's blue badge to remember his name.

"I need to see his face, Matt," he said, fairly steadily. "And if he has a tattoo on his shoulder."

"Push on the plastic to look, I'm not cutting it open for a measly hundred bucks."

Holbrook was resolved to cut the plastic with the rental car key if he had to, but he nodded. His mouth was dry, and tasted of airline peanuts.

Four hours ago in San Francisco his life had still had a purpose, but the phone call from the private detective had effectively shattered it.

"Your friend finally showed up," the detective had said.

"Who is this?" Holbrook had replied impatiently. "What friend? I don't have any friends."

"That's good. I'm talking about your man John Atwater. I'm afraid he's dead. The L.A. County Coroner's Office sent his prints in to the FBI, and they identified him."

Holbrook had found himself sitting on his kitchen floor, watching his coffee cup spin away across the linoleum. "It's—dammit, it's not over yet—there can be errors. With fingerprinting. Did he have the tattoo?"

The man hadn't known that.

Matt paused now beside a steel door; a printed sign on it read STAND CLEAR WHEN

DOOR IS IN MOTION. Holbrook was breathing deeply. Several printed announcements or bulletins were thumbtacked to the wall beside the door, but he couldn't read those.

Matt took hold of the metal handle and slid the door open. Inside, under recessed white lights and roaring ceiling-mounted blowers, long shapes in plastic bags filled metal shelves and lay on narrow wheeled tables. The air in here was very cold.

Matt stepped in and slid the door shut when Holbrook had joined him. "These ones tied with ropes have been autopsied," Matt said, each syllable a puff of steam. "Your man's on the far end, not cut up yet."

Holbrook walked slowly past the angular bagged shapes on the tables, his shoes scuffing on textured strips on the concrete floor. Some of the bodies were wrapped in a silvery plastic, but most of the bags were fairly clear, and through them he could see flesh colors, and here and there patches of red which he assumed were blood. Absently he laid the meaningless clipboard on one of the bags.

The walls were lined with steel shelves divided by partitions, and most of the spaces were occupied by still more plastic wrapped shapes.

Holbrook nodded toward them. “You’ve got room for more.”

“Those shelves on the far wall are for ones that weigh more than two-hundred-and-twenty-five pounds,” commented Matt. “Your pal was up there till they moved him in line here.” He paused beside one of the wheeled tables and waved at the shape on it. “He-e-re’s Johnny.”

Holbrook took a deep breath of the cold air, then stared at the face blurrily visible below the rippled plastic. He hadn’t seen John Atwater for more than ten years, and the man had been athletically trim in those days, while this face was wide. With both hands Holbrook pressed the plastic down against the cheeks, and now the face was narrower and clearly visible. And Holbrook couldn’t pretend that he didn’t recognize it.

He lifted his hands away, then pressed one hand against the plastic over the body’s bare shoulder—and saw the word *THINGS* tattooed in stark sans-serif letters on the pale skin.

Involuntarily he touched his own shoulder; under his jacket and shirt the word *APART* was tattooed in the same lettering. And for a moment he let himself remember the woman whose shoulder had borne the word *FALL*.

He blinked back tears. "You think you're safe now?" he whispered.

The private detective had said that Atwater had been found on a Malibu balcony overlooking the sea, dead of a sudden massive stroke, with a drink beside him and a girlfriend in bed in the room behind him.

Holbrook looked up at Matt. "He died happy."

"We done here? Get your clipboard and let's go." Matt hurried back toward the steel door. "Happy? Well, that's good, isn't it? Come *on*."

Holbrook turned away from the body. "It's…intolerable."

~

Far out of Los Angeles to the east on the old Route 66, late afternoon sunlight threw the shadows of tumbleweeds and an occasional mesquite tree across the two highway lanes that were the only evidence of humanity in an endless flat plain under an empty sky. In the distance, the horizon was the uneven line of the remote Providence Mountains.

Holbrook watched the odometer as he drove, and when he was fourteen miles southeast of the one-gas-station town of Ludlow he slowed the rental Kia and began peering through the windshield for a dirt road slanting off the highway. "Middle of nowhere" seemed to have been an accurate description.

He saw it, or at least saw some cleared track on which tire treads had worn a pair of flattened lines in the sandy dirt. The Kia was only rolling along at about twenty miles per hour now, and he easily steered it off the pavement onto the dirt road.

The car coasted slowly as he kept his foot lifted from the gas pedal. It had been a long, tense drive from Los Angeles—and a longer trip from San Francisco—and he tried to remember when he had last eaten. Last night, in his apartment on Telegraph Hill?

All at once he was shaking, and he gripped the wheel tightly—what if there were no trailer out here at the end of it all, what if the alleged psychic had lied? The phrase *middle of nowhere* seemed suddenly literal, and Holbrook had to resist the impulse to reverse back onto the highway while there still was a highway behind him, while he could still hope to get back to the world, even just the tiny outpost that was now-distant Ludlow. The ragged band that was the remote mountains seemed thinner and even farther away, and for one breathless instant he was sure that if he were to drive across the desert toward them they would recede.

His hand snapped forward defensively, and it hit the button for the radio, and then piano music shook the air-conditioned breeze in the car, at least partly restoring the external world; but after a moment he turned the radio off. He had only heard a couple of bars, and it couldn't have been Ravel's Piano Concerto in G. He could hardly hope to recognize it these days, in any case—it had been Shasta's favorite performance piece, but more than ten years had passed since he had heard her play it.

The engine whined and the car rocked on its shock absorbers as he gave it more gas, and the rear-view mirror showed only dust.

He touched his shoulder, remembering the drunken night in the summer of 2001 when the six members of their close-knit college group had decided to get a set of farewell tattoos.

Shasta and John had just graduated, and two of the others were moving out of state, and after many pitchers of beer at Chasteen's on Sunset, they had all driven over to a tattoo parlor in El Segundo. It had been Tom Holbrook, hopelessly in love with Shasta ever since they had both been freshmen—wondering dejectedly how he might maintain any sort of contact with her after this—who had suggested that each of them be be tattooed with one word from the Yeats line, *Things fall apart, the center cannot hold.* And the alcohol and the melancholy mood of the evening had led them all to agree. The line had one too many words for their group, but none of them had wanted *the* anyway. Pete Calvert, nowadays a school janitor in San Bernardino, had got *CANNOT*; Ed Rocha had got *HOLD*, and at last report he was a real estate millionaire; Dylan Emsley had got *CENTER*, and died in a car crash in '03 at the age of twenty-five.

Shasta DiMaio had got *FALL*. John Atwater had got *THINGS*. Tom Holbrook had wound up with *APART*, which had seemed bleakly appropriate.

The Kia's temperature needle was a bit on the right side of straight up, and Holbrook was ready to switch off the air conditioning and turn on the heater to get a second radiator cooling the engine, when the car crested a low rise and he saw the tan-colored trailer tucked behind a low cluster of cottonwood trees.

It appeared to be corrugated aluminum or fiberglass, and its roof slanted up higher at the far end, with a little window in the long triangle, perhaps to make room for a bunk. There were two wide windows in the flank and a door with a window in it at the near end. It was dusty and its two visible wheels appeared to be flat, but its deliberate lines and angles looked as incongruous in this natural wasteland as a spacecraft on the moon. When Holbrook swerved into the cleared patch in front of it and turned off the car's motor, he could hear the clatter of the trailer's rooftop air conditioner. Feeling unmoored from everything in his life, Holbrook got out of the car and walked through the jarringly hot dry air to the trailer.

The man who opened the trailer's door when Holbrook knocked on it appeared to be in his fifties, thin and clean-shaven, with long gray hair pulled back in a ponytail. He wore jeans and a gray sweatshirt with a nearly faded out peace-sign across the front, and on the cool breeze from inside the trailer Holbrook could smell incense and patchouli oil.

"Holbrook," the man said, in a nasal voice that carried a trace of a British accent. When Holbrook nodded, the man went on, "I'm Martinez, obviously. Whatever it is you want, it will be expensive—nobody ever brings small problems out here." He stood back and waved to the trailer's dim interior. "Sit down."

Holbrook stepped up onto pale blue carpet, and after a few moments he was able to make out upholstered benches along both walls, and wide, curtained windows. Electric light behind pebbled ceiling panels threw a weak yellow glow on the glass-topped table between the benches. The only things on the table were a legal pad, several pencils, and a black laptop computer.

Holbrook edged around the table and sat down. "I want to kill somebody."

Martinez shut the door and slid onto the opposite bench. "By supernatural means, I presume, or you wouldn't have come to me. Well, I can listen, at least. Where is this person?"

Holbrook sighed. "In a plastic bag in the morgue at the Los Angeles County Coroner building."

Martinez sat back and gave him a quizzical look.

"Yes, yes," said Holbrook impatiently, "he's dead, but—that won't do. *I* didn't kill him. And he died happy! Now—I now see that I need to make him cease to exist at all, in any form. He must be—" He lifted a hand and let it drop.

"Really most sincerely dead?" suggested Martinez.

Holbrook didn't smile. "You contact dead people all the time, right? You come highly recommended. So how do you destroy, negate, eradicate, a ghost? And—to the extent that ghosts can be aware of things—I want him to know who did it to him."

Martinez leaned forward to peer at Holbrook. "Who...is he?"

"You might have heard of him. John Atwater. He murdered his wife six years ago, and a year later he was acquitted after a lot of inadmissible evidence and two hung juries. He was a lawyer, and he had high-powered lawyer friends. There were stories in the *L. A. Times*. He went invisible after that; dark, off the grid, in hiding, with a lot of stashed money. When he finally reappeared two days ago, it was because he had died."

In the cool interior of the trailer, Holbrook could smell his own sweat over the scent of patchouli.

"I think I remember it." Martinez leaned back. "The murdered wife had a peculiar name..."

"Shasta."

Holbrook had tried to speak the name levelly, but Martinez nodded slowly. "That's the way of it, eh? You don't want to talk to her?"

"Would she be...available?"

"Well probably not, actually, after six years. They tend to move out from the center, out of Ouija range." He shook his head. "But we can certainly banish the Atwater fellow—block him from manifesting himself, even block him from any awareness of events in…this *mortal coil*. I'll need to find out where they bury him, or at least where they incinerate him, and my expenses will be—"

"But if you banish him, won't he still exist, on the, I don't know, on the other side?"

Martinez shrugged. "For a while, at least, probably. I don't know what becomes of them after they've moved outward, beyond my sphere of perception."

"I want to kill him there. I want him to stop existing there." The trailer shook in a gust of desert wind.

Martinez laughed softly. "My dear fellow, to have any hope of accomplishing that, you'd have to be there yourself. That is to say, dead."

"I'm sure he only went into hiding because he knew I meant to find him and kill him. Now he thinks he's eluded me absolutely, but—I mean to follow him." Holbrook nodded. "Yes, of course, dead."

Martinez was tapping one of the pencils on the tabletop. “Is it…are you certain it’s worth that? He *is dead,* after all.”

Holbrook wiped his damp palms down his thighs. “Nothing else is worth anything.”

Martinez stared at him expressionlessly for several seconds. “I imagine you’re aware that people die every day, hm? Quite a lot of them, actually. Before we go any further, let’s see if we can get a trace on your man.”

He stood up and opened a polished wooden cabinet in the forward wall, and lifted out a square wooden board and a glass jar with a screw-top lid. When he set them on the table, Holbrook saw that letters were printed on the board in a circle, and the jar contained a dozen or so little shiny black insects—peering uneasily, he saw that the scurrying things were earwigs.

“This works better, for a cold call, than the traditional board and sliding planchette,” said Martinez, resuming his seat. “There has to be motion, and the bugs have virtually no wills of their own to interfere with the spirit’s promptings.” He unscrewed the lid of the jar and quickly turned it upside-down on the center of the board, as if he were playing bar dice.

"When I lift it," he told Holbrook, "you say your man's name. It has to be your voice."

Holbrook bared his teeth. "I don't want to talk to him, *converse* with him! Can't you—"

Martinez held up his free hand. "If he answers, we'll hang up. We just want to see if he answers."

Holbrook blew air out through his lips. "Okay. Go."

Martinez snatched the jar away, and Holbrook said, "John Atwater" as the wiggling creatures spread out across the board. Holbrook slid down the bench away from them.

Several of the earwigs had simply stopped, and a few others had crawled off the board and begun exploring the tabletop. None of them moved in any evidently organized or purposeful way. Holbrook wanted to brush back the ones closest to him, but was afraid it might interfere with the procedure.

After a full minute of watching the bugs in tense silence, Martinez said, "No, there's no response from your man. He may be just gone. Ah—wait a moment." He stared at the insects still on the board, and then lifted a hand to point down at several that had clustered near the letter H in the last few seconds. "Aha! I know where he was, as it were, recently, so to speak. It makes sense, since he died in Los Angeles."

Martinez sat back with a sigh, and smiled at Holbrook. "I think we may come to an arrangement. And if we can, I won't require payment in money."

"So you'll…assist?"

"Advise. Guide. Expedite, possibly."

Expedite? thought Holbrook. But how can I object? He's being generous. "Oh. Yes." He exhaled. "Well, I need to know…the geography of the place, the customs, if they have customs. How ghosts interact, what I can do." Holbrook spread his hands. "Everything."

"Yes. Well it's not a particular place; it's more like a lot of different realities simultaneously occupying the same space, just as all sorts of radio frequencies occupy the same air. You find that you've tuned in to one, and you're unaware of the others. But they're all generally described as a vast dome, with new arrivals appearing on the top, and then gradually making their way outward—down the sides. Spirits of Western cultures have traditionally referred to these consensual realities as Purgatory, though these Purgatories don't seem really to correspond to the Roman Catholic idea of that state."

"Consensual realities," said Holbrook, "and I'll tune in to one of them." He frowned doubtfully. "Can decisive things happen in a consensual reality?"

Martinez said drily, "You'd be surprised how much of the substance of *this* world is consensual. Yes, I believe decisive things can happen. Relevant to your purpose, it's generally thought that a mirror can destroy a ghost—not here, but there. It makes a sort of sense; a reflection in a mirror would *be* substantially the ghost who looked into it. They hardly consist of any more than their self-projected appearance, and that frail quantity can apparently jump across to the observed image in the mirror, and the original ghost-figure fades—and if you shatter the mirror then, while his image is in it, you shatter him. There'll be nothing left of him to go on to definition."

"Definition...?"

"That's what they call it when they move out of my perception."

"So a mirror can destroy one."

"They believe so."

"And I can find a mirror there?"

"Not a real mirror, no. There's nothing actually *real,* there. But I suspect that if you hold up your empty hand, or two hands with your fingers outlining a rectangle, and *say* it's a mirror, with some confidence, you may be able to make an adequate substitute appear."

Holbrook frowned. "That's weak."

"Yes," said Martinez. He nodded toward the board on the table. "Your quarry is out of my Ouija range, we got no answer—but the H those bugs gathered around is the distinctive dial-tone, you might say, of a specific Purgatory. There's a fairly articulate, coherent ghost there who calls himself Hubcap Pete. I can generally raise him. Unlike most of his kind, he has been a resident, if you will, of his particular Purgatory for at least ten years of our time, and his gets a lot of local expirations—I think he lived in Los Angeles, or died there anyway. When you, er, arrive, he'll probably be willing to explain the place and its ways to you."

Arrive there, thought Holbrook with a shiver. *When I arrive there.* He forced a casual tone into his voice and said, "He doesn't stray from the top of the *dome,* this Hubcap guy?"

"I believe he travels all over it, actually. There are apparent highways. He's forever driving a virtual car of some sort. In fact I suspect it's his attention that sustains this particular Purgatory gyre or wavelength. Now listen carefully, and remember—for this expedition, you and I will be able to communicate via Ouija software, just as we'll shortly be communicating with him, and the payment I ask is that you find out who Pete was when he was alive. Where he lived, what his name was, when he died, as much as you can learn."

"He won't tell you himself?"

"No."

"Why do you want to know who he was?"

"Why, I want to lay flowers on his grave, don't I? Adopt his dogs, finish his crossword puzzles? What do you care? Only do this for me."

Holbrook sat back and closed his eyes for a moment, resting his head against the curtained window behind him. "Okay." He opened his eyes when he heard Martinez tapping the computer keyboard. "You can get online out here?"

"No," said Martinez absently, "there's no DSL out here, and with satellite internet the ping time is annoying." He glanced up. "Not the sort of online you mean, anyway. And this has to be done well away from populated areas, in any case—Pete is what they call an over-easy spirit, meaning that he died while he was actually engaged in contact with the afterworld. He already had one foot in the door, you might say, half his weight there, so the crossover wasn't as traumatic and damaging for him as it is for most ghosts. He still has a good deal of mental power. We'll see to it that you're an 'over-easy' too. But such ghosts are dangerous to summon. Sometimes lethal."

Holbrook managed a smile. "He might kill me?"

"Unlikely. You seem firmly in touch with your surroundings, if a bit stressed at the moment. But you'll feel the mental impact when I get Pete on the line, and 'over-easy' ghosts like him have been known to bump a living soul right out of its body, if it was shaky or inexperienced, and take its place. The ancient Jewish mystics called such entities *dybbuks*. I'm fairly sure that my man Pete would never do that deliberately, but such ghosts *are* drawn to weak souls. Hence my remote location. Nobody should ever use Ouija in a populated area."

"So I should do my dying here?" *Tonight?* Holbrook thought. He was all at once aware of his heartbeat, the pulse in his temples, the seesaw flex of his lungs.

Martinez was still tapping away at the keyboard. "Hm? Oh—yes, definitely, if I can get hold of Pete." He nodded toward the door. "It's a big desert, no morgue for you. Part of the service."

Holbrook swallowed to quell a surge of nausea. It *is* worth it, he told himself. And after I've broken the mirror with Atwater in it, I'll look in a mirror myself, and it'll break when I disappear and it hits the pavement. If I can conjure up a couple of mirrors.

"Is there pavement in Purgatory?" he asked.

Martinez looked up impatiently. "There seem to be streets, so I suppose there's pavement. The spirits say they walk around. It's just consensual gravity, too, at least at the top of the dome. Ghosts don't have near enough mass to have any measurable weight."

"Ghosts have *any* mass?"

"Of course they do, or they'd move at the speed of light." Martinez pushed his chair back. "Now then—I'm about to call Hubcap Pete. He communicates via some sort of keypad on his end, but in order to leapfrog over the barrier from the other side, his words need to have some physical manifestation here, motion, like my scurrying bugs or the moving planchette on traditional Ouija boards; pixels on a monitor aren't macro enough. So I route him through TTS, text-to-speech software, and sound waves in air and vibrating eardrums are agitation enough to do the trick. He'll be a synthesized voice, lacking intonation and stress. And in order to maintain himself, his precariously autonomous self, he always talks in rhyme when he's talking across the mortal gulf. A counter-entropy move, you see. You remember how you'll pay me?"

"Information about who Hubcap Pete was," said Holbrook, "when he was alive."

"Right. Let's have at it then—put off, and sitting well in order, smite."

Martinez stood up and opened the wooden cabinet again, and a moment later he stepped toward the door, hefting a big black gun. Holbrook's heart was thumping hard in his chest as he made himself look squarely at the weapon, and he saw that it was a pump-action 12-gauge shotgun, with a pistol grip instead of a shoulder stock. Only after a shocked moment did Holbrook notice that the man had also fetched from the cabinet a roll of Saran Wrap.

"Would you bring the laptop?" Martinez said. "Obviously we do this outside."

Holbrook couldn't immediately stand up. "Whoa, with a *shotgun?* Wouldn't something like…I don't know, cyanide…?"

"Induce confusion and unpredictable behavior? Yes. Almost certainly break your connection with Pete? Yes. Instantaneous is better." Martinez opened the door, and a hot breeze swept into the trailer, spicy with the scent of sage. The light outside was the amber glow of sunset. "You can still reconsider, naturally, and simply pay me for this past twenty-minute consultation."

Holbrook thought of Shasta as he had last seen her—she and John had been in L.A. for a week in 2006, and she had invited him to join them for an early dinner at Mastro's. Shasta had been thinner than he remembered, with new lines under her eyes and down her cheeks. John had looked fit and tanned, and had paid the whole tab with a Platinum American Express card. Shasta had kissed Holbrook, perhaps wistfully, when they left.

And he remembered the murder trial—one of the exhibits had been a mannequin wearing a brown-spotted sweater of Shasta's, with wooden dowels projecting like arrows from the chest to indicate the paths of the bullets.

"No," he said, getting to his feet and reaching for the laptop, "I'm on board." He followed Martinez out through the door. The rattle of the rooftop air-conditioner was louder outside.

Martinez led him around to the shaded far side of the trailer, where a wrought iron table and four chairs stood on a cleared patch of sandy dirt. The table and chairs had once been painted white, but were flecked with rust now. Beyond them stood a Jeep half covered by a blue tarpaulin, and beyond that the desert stretched away in copper light and long shadows toward the distant mountains.

"You take the chair facing away from the trailer," Martinez said. He laid the shotgun and the roll of Saran Wrap on the iron table, then took the laptop from Holbrook and sat down on the other side.

Martinez opened the computer and tapped some more keys, and now he spoke into it.

"Pete? Come over here." The desert breeze drew low veils of sand around the sides of the trailer, and a hawk hung in the purple sky. "Pete? I want you to meet a fellow."

Holbrook sat down slowly. He found that he was hoping Hubcap Pete wouldn't make the connection, and then he despised himself for that hope. *She* died, he thought; can't you?

Abruptly his view of the table and Martinez faded; a moment later he could see clearly again, and he hastily wiped his mouth and blinked around, reminding himself of where he was.

"He's on," whispered Martinez. "You felt his arrival, didn't you?"

Then a flat, not-quite-continuous voice buzzed out of the laptop's speaker. Holbrook had to lean closer to hear it clearly.

"I know why your boy came…he's been looking for some dame." After a pause, the voice went on, "Has he found her…is this just fan mail from some flounder."

"No," said Holbrook, glancing from the black cover of the computer to Martinez, and back. He was sweating, still disoriented. "No, I'm looking for the man who killed her. His name is Atwater, John Atwater."

Martinez whispered, "They prefer not to use—"

"We mostly don't tell each other who we were," said Hubcap Pete. "It's too much of a lure."

"—their real names there," Martinez finished.

For a moment the air conditioner rattled more loudly in a gust of hot wind.

Holbrook pressed on, "How do I find a ghost, a spirit, there? Will you be able to direct me?"

"You do not—" began the voice; and then it stopped.

Holbrook held his breath, staring at the laptop on the iron table. After a few seconds he let his breath out and looked up at Martinez, raising his eyebrows.

"Wait a bit," said Martinez. "He's probably just going through a tunnel." He met Holbrook's puzzled gaze. "I told you he drives all the time. Do you have any identifying marks? For when I call you. Spirits there won't know your name."

Holbrook hesitated, then lifted his shoulder. "A tattoo. It says 'Apart.'"

"That'll do fine. It'll probably make itself visible. You're vulnerable if the ghosts know your real name, so don't—"

But the voice from the computer was speaking again: "Well…was that all you wanted me to tell."

"We didn't hear your answer," said Martinez to the computer. "Please repeat."

"I said, You do not need me to direct…call him like you called me collect."

"No," said Holbrook, "I mean if I'm there, where you and he are, can you tell me how to find him there?"

"Ha ha ha," came three measured syllables from the computer's speakers. "You would have to die…to get here guy."

Martinez pushed back his chair and stood up. "That's his plan, Pete. He wants to be an over-easy ghost, like what you are." He picked up the roll of Saran Wrap, unreeled a couple of feet of the clear film and tore it off.

The synthesized voice said, "Is that true… what he says about you."

Martinez draped the film over the computer and tucked the edges under it. He gestured for Holbrook to keep talking.

"That's right," Holbrook said hoarsely.

He doesn't want to get blood and brains on his computer, he thought. He's going to shoot me from behind; from up close—there's hardly four feet between the trailer wall and the back of my head. More loudly, he went on, "Yes, it's true."

The voice from the computer was not muffled by the plastic film. "Not likely you find him among all the expansions…in our father's halfway house are many mansions."

Martinez spoke. "We believe he's in the same mansion you're in, Pete."

After a pause, "Please think again son," said the voice from the laptop's speaker, "this thing can't be undone."

Martinez leaned down and whispered to Holbrook, "Keep him talking. This won't take but a moment." He reached over and picked up the shotgun, then stepped behind Holbrook's chair.

Holbrook's hands were shaking, and he stuffed them into his jacket pockets. His vision seemed to have narrowed, and a high keening wailed in his mind, and he couldn't take a deep breath.

He made himself think again of the mannequin with the dowels protruding from its chest.

"I want to do it," he said. "Now. While I'm talking to you."

He heard Hubcap Pete's flat voice say, "You're a chump...but hang onto my shirt tail sonny and jump."

From behind him, Holbrook heard the fast clatter and click of a shell being chambered in the shotgun.

Holbrook's teeth were clenched so hard that his jaw hinges ached. This call is collect, he thought. This is on your credit card, John. You're paying for all of this.

"I'm holding on," he grated. "Don't drop me."

Two endless seconds passed.

Then with a silent but incomprehensibly profound cleaving he was kicked forward, out across the desert, and the low hills and scrub brush hurtled past beneath him. He tried to blink against an expected headwind, but in fact there didn't seem to be any air around him at all, and he didn't have eyelids in any case. He realized that his vision swept a full 360 degrees—he perceived the mountains rushing up at him and the trailer receding in an infinite distance; and the dark sky and the racing sand were simultaneously visible too.

There was no sound at all, until he heard a voice say, "I'll drop you near the town square,"—and it was a human voice, gruff and deep, not the synthesized voice any longer.

Holbrook stumbled, and a street tilted itself so that he didn't fall.

"Want it or not?" said a dim figure sitting behind a counter in front of him. On the counter was a beige plastic knob the size of a quarter, with string wrapped around a short metal post on one side of it.

Holbrook looked around quickly, and he knew there was air because he was panting; and he had eyes again, because he was blinking. The breeze smelled of diesel fumes and was very cold; and though he saw that he was now wearing only a damp T-shirt and ragged cut-off jeans and sneakers, it was not the chill, but relief—to see that he actually had a body—that made him shiver. He stood in a narrow street between tall buildings; at one moment their walls were featureless, but as he shifted his head he saw that they were peppered with tiny hinged windows all opening and shutting rapidly, and then the walls were smooth again. Looking up, he saw gray clouds churning in the gap between the angular rooftops.

He could feel a rapid heartbeat in his chest. I'm okay? he thought tentatively. I still exist, at least.

He turned back to the figure that had spoken—it was apparently a woman, almost completely hidden under a profusion of multicolored shawls—and he pointed at the little knob on the counter.

He found that he was able to speak. "What is it?" he asked dizzily.

"I think it's a yo-yo," the figure answered.

Holbrook picked it up, and for a moment it was as light as a shred of styrofoam; then his hand sagged as it assumed several pounds of weight. If it was a yo-yo it was awfully small, and one side of it was missing.

A white-haired man in khaki shorts and a Polo shirt jostled Holbrook and leaned in over the counter, and said something to him that sounded like "Take it apart."

Holbrook laid the plastic knob back down on the counter and stepped back, across a two-inch sidewalk into the street. "Not," he said carefully, "today. Thank you."

The pavement felt spongy for a moment, but when he turned and began walking, his sneakers scuffed solidly against it.

A cold hand caught at his elbow. He turned and saw that the old man in the Polo shirt had followed him and was insistently waving what appeared to be a white patent leather boot with an antenna sticking out of the top. "I think it's for you, Apart," he said.

Holbrook peered more closely at the object and saw that it was an old Motorola mobile phone from the 1980s. He took it from the old man and held it up to his ear.

"Uh," he said. He had not stopped panting. "Who is—"

"Rhyme, remember," interrupted a voice from up near the antenna. "Apart, this is Martinez. Type an answer in whatever sort of keypad you see. It has to rhyme, remember. Apart, this is—"

Holbrook held the bulky old instrument away, and he saw that the keys on the inner side of it bore letters but no numbers.

He tapped the keys and the space bar for GUY JUST GAVE ME THIS PHONE and then IM NOT ALONE

He gasped when he tapped the E key, for in that instant the gray daylight was extinguished and he could see only a dark plain with one spark in the center of it; but a moment later the narrow street surged back into visibility around him, and the old man in the Polo shirt was still frowning at him.

"Ah!" came Martinez' voice from the phone's speaker, "good, good! Give that person some money for the phone, keep it with you if you can. But spell out words how you want them pronounced—and you don't have to rhyme when you're talking to others of your—now—sort. Find Pete."

The phone was silent. Holbrook dug in his pants pocket and pulled out a roll of bills. For a few seconds the denominations were hard to read, then he saw that they were all hundred-dollar bills. He peeled one off, with difficulty, and handed it to the old man.

"Did you call me...Apart?" Holbrook asked. He flexed his hand, which was tingling as if he had slept on it.

The old man scowled and pointed at Holbrook's shoulder; and when Holbrook glanced sideways and down, he saw that the black letters of his tattoo were clearly visible through the T-shirt's damp, threadbare fabric—the letters even seemed to be bigger.

Holbrook took a deep breath and let it out, and the cityscape seemed to settle down, the silhouettes of buildings and streetlamp poles straightening out and subsiding to vertical.

Now other figures were visible in the shadowed street—two children were hopping past, each with one leg in a canvas sack, though as they receded they looked more like one three-legged child; a couple of shadowy young men shook hands in a doorway opposite, and kept on doing it; a cluster of teenage girls hurried by with faint cries like parakeets, and after a few steps he lost sight of them and could see only an old woman hobbling away—and Holbrook became aware that the old man in khaki shorts was still frowning up at him.

"I got a Bluetooth!" said the old man. "But it's fake, I made it out of candy wrappers." He stepped back. "You think you're so big. You say you got this, and you got that, and you got this shiny telephone that works."

Holbrook's teeth were cold in the chilly breeze that funneled down the street, and he closed his mouth.

"Uh," he said finally, "what? The telephone? You gave it to me." The two young men were still shaking hands, with no sign of stopping soon, or ever. He added, "And I gave you a hundred bucks for it."

"Monopoly money. And the call was for you." For a moment the man's hair was dark brown, and slicked back in a 1950s-style ducktail; then it was sparse and white again. "I never get calls. I'm as good as you."

The mobile phone had softened in Holbrook's grip—his fingers were sinking into it, wetly, and he opened his hand and let it fall to the cobblestones. It broke into quivering pieces like an upended panful of vanilla pudding.

"Holy Toledo," exclaimed the old man. "Now you got no phone at all." He took Holbrook's hand and led him several yards down the street, past the shoulder of a building on the left and into brighter light.

Holbrook freed his hand and stopped. They were in one corner of a broad square now, between stark concrete Bauhaus-style buildings with black windows and empty gray balconies. A few evidently human figures were visible near a fountain out toward the center of the square, and a bridge like a Roman aqueduct was visible between two of the buildings on the far side, under a turbulent ash-colored sky.

Holbrook quailed at the volume of the open space, after the close walls of the street behind them.

"Do you," he said quietly, "know a guy called Hubcap Pete?"

"Sure. Watch the bridge there and you'll see him. Can I have another hundred bucks?"

"In a second." Holbrook peered at the bridge in the distance, but though he saw several rectangles like semi-trailers moving across the top of it, he didn't see any sort of car.

"I need to find somebody," he went on. "How do I find somebody, here? No, not Pete, somebody else—his real name is John Atwater." He pulled the roll of bills out of his pocket and tugged one free.

The old man snatched it from him. "The stud," he said, nodding. "You want to find the stud."

"Is that what he says?" Holbrook's face was real enough to feel suddenly hot. "He's a liar, he abused his wife—"

His companion giggled and looked around, though none of the other figures were nearby. "No, it's how you find a stud—you knock along the wall, right? Boom boom boom boom rap! There's no use putting a nail in the plaster if there's no stud behind it. You knock in all directions till it sounds different, and you know that's where it is."

"Oh!" Holbrook exhaled and made himself relax as he stuffed the rest of the money back into his pocket. "How do I…*knock on the wall,* then?" The old man's face wrinkled in a baffled frown, and Holbrook went on quickly, "I get it, it's like knocking on a wall to find the wood, the stud, behind the plaster—so how do I do that to find somebody here?"

"Well you call his real name, don't you?" the man said irritably. "What did you think? The fountain there is the top of the bell, you can face in all directions from there."

"Okay. Thanks. Uh, keep the change." Holbrook began hesitantly shuffling forward, away from the high walls.

Behind him, the old man shouted, "You got a shadow! *I* got no shadow!"

The pavement of the square was bricks fitted together in a herringbone pattern, and when Holbrook glanced down, he saw that there was indeed a blurry patch of shade on the red bricks around his sneakers. Well, he thought, I'm an over-easy ghost. I bet I'm not likely to turn into a three-legged child or a group of teenagers.

The sea of bricks was perceptibly rippled in concentric rings around the fountain; the ripples bent around the corner of the building behind him. Holbrook made his way out across the square, stepping carefully over the humped rows of brick. The ridges were lower toward the center of the square.

Water cascaded from the bowl at the top of the white stone fountain and fell down through rings of stone petals into a wide pool with a knee-high coping. Children were splashing in the pool, but Holbrook had already developed a reluctance to look too closely at the inhabitants of Purgatory.

The spray from the fountain was stingingly cold when Holbrook had got to within a yard of the pool, and he held out his hands and tried forcefully to imagine a quilted jacket to pull on over his clinging T-shirt—a well-remembered jacket that he had once owned, red nylon, with an overlapping zipper—and for a moment a wisp of red fog curled around his fingers before blowing away.

Abandoning the effort, he hugged himself against the wind and turned away from the fountain. "John Atwater!" he called across the square.

He felt no change, and there was no response, not even an echo from the Soviet-looking apartment building fifty yards away. He was still shivering, and now his leg itched and he couldn't scratch it properly through the denim.

He edged several steps to the right, and tried calling Atwater's name again. Again there was no response, though the children in the fountain splashed water on him, having perhaps heard only the last two syllables of his call.

He didn't waste breath in cursing them, but stepped a yard farther to the right, and this time called the hated name toward a tall cement cube that might have been a prison. No faces appeared at the narrow windows, and there was still no echo. Holbrook paused to scratch his leg again, though the itching persisted.

Holbrook was sweating in spite of the cold. *What if he's not here?* he thought. *What if I died for nothing?*

After six more shuffling, shivering, hoarsening tries, he was facing the gap in the buildings through which he could see the distant bridge—and now he saw a brightly lime-green car moving across the span. Even from this distance he could make out its tall tailfins, and while he watched it move, all the frail traces of other colors vanished from the drab cityscape.

And when he again cried, "John Atwater!" the warehouse to the left of the gap quivered on its unguessable foundations, and for a few moments it was a one-story brick building with curtained windows—and, as if borrowing color from the passing distant car, green-leafed magnolia trees stood on either side of the open front door. And it seemed closer.

Then it was just the warehouse across the square, its streaked concrete walls and spinning rooftop air vents as solid-seeming as before.

Ping, Holbrook thought.

He had recognized the briefly visible smaller building; it was Chasteen's, the restaurant in which the six of them used to spend long evenings over bock beer and

Turkish coffee. On the last night they had all gathered there, shortly before deciding to get the group tattoo, Holbrook had drunkenly recited to Shasta two lines from an A. E. Housman poem—*May will be fine next year, as like as not: /Oh aye, but then we shall be twenty-four.* And in fact they had both been twenty-three then, and by the following May Shasta was married to John and living far away.

Find the stud, Holbrook thought; he's in that direction. He stepped away from the fountain and hurried across the square toward the street that opened beside the warehouse.

As he stepped over one of the higher curved pavement ridges he glanced down, and then paused. The uptilted bricks had fallen aside at one point, and he noticed a square gray box wedged in the gap. He took a moment to crouch and peer at it—it was a model of a building, with tiny windows on its sides and a cluster of miniature air-conditioning ducts on its roof. It didn't move at all when he reached down and tugged at it, and he only succeeded in crushing in one side with his thumb, so he straightened and hurried away.

The street alongside the warehouse was paved with asphalt, and broadened out as it extended away from the square. Within a block it took on a residential look—the buildings on either side were only two or three stories tall, set well back from the curbs, with bay windows and forests of TV antennas on the roofs, and many of the front yards were cluttered with various sorts of litter, among which Holbrook noted mismatched couch cushions and piles of broken crockery. People were picking through the stuff, and Holbrook concluded that these were yard sales. He could hear someone down the street trying to get a car started, and he caught different smells on the air now—tobacco, and corn tortillas, and chlorine. A profusion of shoes with the laces tied together swung like little pendulums on street-spanning cables, and beyond them the monochrome silhouette of an airplane moved across the sky in quick jumps, like a spider.

Abruptly the asphalt shivered under Holbrook's feet, and he hopped sideways to keep his balance. A woman in a pink skirt and jacket who had been standing on the curb ahead of him was now sitting in the street; when the shaking subsided he hurried over to her, glancing nervously at the cables and shoes swinging overhead.

"We shouldn't be under the power lines," he said, extending a hand to help her up. "There might be aftershocks."

Blonde hair had fallen across the woman's face, and she brushed it aside with one hand and took Holbrook's hand with the other. Her face, blinking up at him in surprise, was smooth—Holbrook guessed that she was in her early twenties. When he pulled her to her feet, her weight was hardly more than he would have expected from just lifting her velvet skirt and jacket.

"Aftershocks?" she said, and Holbrook almost flinched, for her voice was like the squeak of iron nails being pried out of wood. "Where you been, honey? There aren't any earthquakes." She didn't release his hand, and squeezed it several times.

"So what was that?" asked Holbrook. He glanced upward again. "A bomb?"

"The bell has to stretch when it grows out, doesn't it? And it has to grow out to make up for the bits that fall off the bottom edge, where the gravity's real and hard. I stay up here." She was still squeezing his hand. "And there's no electricity in those wires, and they can't fall anyway." She looked down at his feet. "You're a diplomatic, aren't you, Mister Apart? A real big spender, didn't go through Customs." She laughed, a sound like glass breaking. "Listen, take me with you—I can have a body temperature with the right fella, and I know a million songs."

Holbrook realized that she had seen his faint shadow on the asphalt. "I don't know where I'm going, I'm just looking for a guy—"

"Don't take *him*, what do you want to take him for? You're not *queer*, are you? Take me!"

"I'm not taking anyone anywhere!" He tugged, but she still gripped his hand.

"Aww, why go alone? I could wash your hair, teach you to juggle, remind you of things—"

Holbrook looked around him at the street; the visible people had resumed picking among the junk laid out in the yards, and the starter motor was still whining farther down the street, and he remembered her saying *I stay up here*. "For God's sake, where is it you think I'm going?"

"Don't tease me, honey—everybody knows you over-easy fellas can jump right off the bell and start over again in real life, as a baby."

"What, like reincarnation?"

"That's it. We can be a couple while you do it. I like you."

"A couple—" Her jacket was unbuttoned, and he could see that she wasn't wearing anything under it. "A couple," he repeated.

Then, for a moment so brief that she didn't notice it herself, three wooden dowels stood out from her breasts, and when Holbrook jerked back he pulled his hand free of hers.

"I," he stammered, stepping away from her, "I've got something to do. I'm sorry." He turned and began walking quickly away down the street, the breeze chilling his sweaty face.

From behind him he heard her despairing wail, "I could have been your twin!"

He waved without looking back.

A moving shape in the street caught his eye, and when he had walked closer he saw that it was a gleaming black motorized wheelchair with a skeletal man elaborately strapped into it. The man's finger flicked back and forth on the control lever, and the wheelchair buzzed forward a yard, then back, then a yard to the side, and at one point Holbrook had to hop to avoid being bumped by the wide tires. Peering more closely, he saw that the man's eyes were tightly shut and that a pair of headphones were clamped onto the bald head. A faint darkness of shade moved back and forth on the pavement beside the wheelchair, but Holbrook couldn't think of anything to be gained by distracting the man, and he hurried past.

Before he had taken twenty long steps away from the bobbing wheelchair, he heard "*Apart!*" called from somewhere in front of him; and the source seemed oddly close to his face, though the nearest person was a man sitting behind the wheel of an old white Dodge Dart a dozen yards ahead. The starter motor chattered on, and the car shook, and smoke and fragments of birds' nests blew out of the exhaust pipe, but the engine still didn't start.

Over the noise of it he again heard a voice call the word tattooed on his shoulder.

He blinked around at the preoccupied figures on the street, none of whom were close to him or looking at him, and then he walked over to the Dodge. The driver's side window was cranked down, and the man in the car was opening and closing his mouth, perhaps cursing.

"Excuse me," said Holbrook loudly, leaning down to peer in. The man behind the wheel was wearing a suit and tie, and his white shirt was blotted with sweat.

"It's an emergency, officer," the man gasped without looking up from the dashboard. His hand kept the ignition key twisted to the right, and the harsh noise continued. "My daughter's wedding—"

"Did you hear—" Holbrook began, then realized that this man couldn't have heard anything above the unceasing snarling of the starter motor.

"My daughter," the man said through clenched teeth. "It'll all be okay between us if I can get there."

Holbrook stepped back, shrugged helplessly, then turned and resumed walking down the street. He was leaning back slightly as he walked, though the street ahead didn't visibly deviate from level; the sensation was as if the whole world were tilting. The buildings on either side didn't quite stand up at right angles to the pavement now, but were tilted a few degrees in the direction of the square behind him.

Soon a low buzz was louder than the receding starter motor, and when Holbrook glanced to the side he saw a little girl on a skateboard slanting toward him across the mottled gray asphalt.

"You're the guy, I bet," she piped as she swerved to a stop beside him, her dark pigtails flying. "The guy the jukebox is calling for." She glanced at his shoulder and nodded, then waved toward a hot-dog-and-bun-shaped stuccoed structure ahead on the right; on a sign over its long windows was painted LOSSAGE SAUSAGE.

Again Holbrook heard the word *Apart* shiver the air in front of him, and the sound did seem to come from the direction of the odd little diner.

"Like that," the girl said. She was wearing a yellow gingham dress with white ribbons, and Holbrook thought she looked dressed up for a birthday party.

"Probably," he said. "Uh, do you know why it's doing that?"

"Somebody from the original world wants to talk to you, I guess. Everybody who's staying up here is retarded—you're smart to be heading downhill."

Holbrook looked back the way he'd come. "That guy in the car—*that's* not Hubcap Pete, is it?"

The girl shook her head solemnly. "No, Hubcap Pete never turns his big green car off. *That* guy? *Him?* He's been there for years—his car won't ever start, and you can't even talk to him. I've tried to, a lot. He's never gonna go down to graduation." She shrugged. "I probably wouldn't either, if I was him."

"Graduation?"

"You know, when you fly off the bottom edge of the bell and find out what grade you're in. I bet *he'd* just be in detention—he was real mean to his daughter."

Holbrook was glancing toward the diner, and so it was only in his peripheral vision that he saw the girl's silhouette flicker and become taller; when he looked back at her she was the little girl in pigtails.

She pushed off, crouching on the skateboard to gain speed downhill. "See you later," she called back, "if we're in the same class!"

Holbrook watched her ride away down the street, then sighed and began trudging toward the red-and-brown-painted diner.

He heard scratchy music from inside the place as he approached the screen door, and when he was still a couple of steps away from the threshold the door was pushed open as a heavyset man in a football jersey stumbled out, fell, and began rolling quietly down the pavement; Holbrook caught the door and stepped inside.

The interior was narrow, with red vinyl booths along the wall opposite the close streetside windows, and he could hear a tired disco rhythm from the glowing jukebox at the uphill end of the place. The warmer air smelled of sauerkraut. He stepped past half a dozen translucent figures slouched in the booths, and just as he stopped in front of the jukebox the vague music paused and a voice from the speaker said, "Apart."

He was not surprised to see that the buttons on the front panel were the twenty-six letters of the alphabet and a space bar. His hand was tingling again, but he stretched his fingers and then typed out, ITS ME WHAT OF THEE.

And when he pushed the E button for the last time, his narrow surroundings dimmed, and for a moment he again saw a broad dark plain with one spark visible on it, as he had when he'd tapped a message into the big mobile phone by the square; then the gaudy housing of the jukebox drove the glimpse away.

"You'll compromise yourself with such lousy rhymes," said Martinez's voice from the jukebox. "I'm glad I finally caught you—you're nearly out of range, I've been trying for days."

It's been days, there? thought Holbrook. He breathed deeply to shake off a wave of dizziness, wondering where his real body might be—his no doubt headless body. He quickly scratched his scalp here.

Martinez went on from the tinny speaker, "You haven't stayed in touch with Hubcap Pete, damn it. I was just talking to him, and now he says he's been the verifier there long enough, he's ready to jump."

Holbrook lowered his hand and forced himself not to think about a mound of newly-turned dirt in some remote Mojave desert arroyo. Don't look back, he told himself. *You* don't *need* Pete—finding Atwater is all that matters now, it's all that's left, and you've got a line on him even without Pete's help.

As if he'd read his mind, Martinez said, "Apart, Pete is the verifier—he's an alert spirit that's always circulating around that Purgatory, observing every district of it, validating it all. If he jumps, if he goes away, that Purgatory gyre is likely to wobble and then simply implode. The moon may exist even if nobody's looking at it, but I'm afraid this Purgatory won't, if Pete stops looking at it."

Holbrook bared his teeth, and his face had suddenly gone cold in spite of the warm air. It can't implode before I find Atwater! he thought. And somehow show him a mirror, and then break it.

He thought rapidly for a few moments, then typed, I SHOULD TALK HIM OUT

OF IT THEN YOUR SAYING AND WITHOUT ANY FURTHER DELAYING.

"That's much better. Yes. I probably won't be able to contact you again for a while, till you get back to the center, but I told him he should hold off because you had something important to tell him. Don't ask, I have no suggestions. And remember what you're doing for me in exchange for all this!"

In exchange for you blowing my head off, thought Holbrook. But, "I remember," he muttered, and he typed, WORRY NOT I HAVENT FORGOT.

The jukebox shook, and then there was just the listless disco music quivering in the speaker.

A lanky-haired young man smoking a cigarette had sidled up while Holbrook had been listening to Martinez's voice, and now he spoke up. "You and me," he said, "we can always get reincarnated if this place collapses. We're over-easies, right? Not like the rest of these losers." He drew on the cigarette, and the tip glowed.

Holbrook noticed that smoke was now leaking from the young man's chest and from under his jaw; and he was sure that if they were outside, the young man would cast no patch of shadow. You're an over-easy only in your dreams, kid, he thought.

Still, Holbrook wanted to know about this alleged reincarnation option. It would be an unlooked-for salvation to be able to live a human life again, after eradicating Atwater here.

Looking past his companion toward the door, Holbrook said, "You sure you know how, sonny?"

"Duh! I was in and out of courtrooms all the time. Ask anybody. You just jump off, or fall off, and when you're arraigned you plead *nolo contendere—nolo contendere* spelled backward is reincarnation."

"Uh—no it's not."

"Yes it is. I heard it on the radio."

Holbrook shrugged. This was useless, and his leg was itching again; walking would be a relief. "Well, I'll see you in a nursery sometime, maybe, back in the original world."

The young man followed him down the aisle to the screen door, but stayed inside when Holbrook stepped out onto the street.

"I'm, uh, not supposed to be out in direct sunlight," he muttered, edging back toward the booths. "Skin cancer."

Direct sunlight? thought Holbrook, glancing at the churning overcast sky; but he waved and started away down the increasingly tilted street in the direction the girl on the skateboard had gone.

He passed a row of 1920s-style bungalows, most of them draped in canvas tents as if for termite extermination, and then he appeared to be in a little business district—he saw car repair garages with huge balloons in the shapes of apes and Santa Clauses bobbing on the roofs, and neon-lit smokeshops, and a movie theater with a dozen inflated tube men out front flailing their long arms around the letterless marquee. Holbrook could hear screaming from inside, and he wondered uneasily what movie might be playing.

At one point he crouched as another earthquake—or dome stretching—shook the street. He held his breath, hoping it wasn't the first shock of this Purgatory collapsing; and when the pavement and buildings remained standing, he straightened and hastily called, "John Atwater!"

Ahead of him and to the left, the multicolored boomerang-shaped buttresses of a car wash vanished, and Holbrook saw the brick walls and curtained windows and sidewalk magnolia trees of Chasteen's. And he was able to take several steps in that direction before the mirage vanished and the car wash reappeared.

I'm getting closer, he thought tensely; Atwater may be only a couple of streets away.

He stepped into the recessed doorway of a pawnshop and held up his left hand with the thumb extended; his right hand was still tingling uncomfortably.

"I'm holding a mirror," he whispered. He tried to make himself feel the edges of a rectangle of glass, and squinted at the space between his fingers, hoping to see the shop door reflected in it. And for a moment he was holding a flat white object; it felt rubbery, but it was a vastly better result than the jacket he had tried to imagine beside the fountain in the square.

The object faded to nothing after a few seconds, so he shook his fingers, took a deep breath and tried again—this time the rectangle that appeared felt like hard plastic, and in it he saw Martinez's trailer in the Mojave desert.

"Getting there," he told himself after it faded, and he pushed out of the recessed doorway and resumed walking down the street. The pavement was now so steep that he had to set his feet carefully to avoid sliding—though when he glanced back the way he'd come, the street ascended straight as a ruler, with no evident change in inclination along its visible length.

Ahead of him now were terraces tilted toward him, and he guessed that if he were standing there they would seem to be level. The Purgatory bell was evidently subject to optical illusions.

Another street crossed this descending one, and he made his way to the corner and turned to the left, walking on pavement that now slanted down at his right. At least the tattoo parlors and bars that he was passing, though set higher on one side, were all vertical. The chilly breeze here smelled of gasoline and bananas. He walked along the downhill side of the street, swinging around streetlamp poles and watching the crumbling curb under his feet.

He was panting and shivering in the breeze, and when he looked up at the high side of the street and again saw the brick wall and curtained windows of Chasteen's, he paused, watching the little restaurant and waiting for it to disappear. And he had stared at it for nearly thirty seconds before remembering that he had not called *John Atwater* this time.

This time it was not a mirage—this was the place his call had shown him and led him to, as real as any other place in Purgatory.

11

*I*s he *in* there? thought Holbrook.

He forced himself to take one slow step after another up the asphalt slope.

Holbrook knew that his real heart was stopped and cold in an unmarked grave in the original world, but he could nevertheless feel a pulse pounding in his temples, and he was dizzy enough to keep his hands spread to the sides as he walked up to the higher curb.

He remembered the broad face he had dimly seen through clear plastic at the Los Angeles Coroner's morgue. It seemed a very long time ago.

Will I shortly be looking into that face?

Atwater had still been handsome and fit-looking when Holbrook had had dinner with him and Shasta at Mastro's in 2006. Holbrook had at that time been a proofreader at a throwaway advertising paper in nearby Culver City, and Atwater had pretended to be very interested in hearing all the details of the job, while Shasta had just looked out the window and taken rapid sips of her Manhattan. Three years later she had been in a roped bag in the Coroner's building.

Up on the level sidewalk now, Holbrook turned around and looked down at the sloping skyline of Purgatory. He could see towers and steeples at a distance of at least a mile; all of them were tilted toward him. Clearly he must be on the descending skirt of the bell—but he had noticed no curvature of the pavement since leaving the fountain in the square, no convexity.

He dismissed the puzzle and turned to face the front door of Chasteen's. The round stained glass window and the iron latch were exactly as he remembered, and the door swung inward when he squeezed the latch and pushed. Familiar smells of tomato sauce and fennel and garlic rode the puff of warm air from the lamplit interior, and he saw a pitcher of dark beer on the table the six of them had customarily occupied.

He had closed the door against the cold breeze outside and taken two steps across the wooden floor when a chair scraped at the other end of the dining room and a voice called loudly, "Excuse me, you got a problem?"

Holbrook braced himself and then faced the figure that was now standing back there by the fireplace; but even in the relative dimness he could see that it was not John Atwater.

"Dylan?" said Holbrook softly. "Dylan Emsley!" Immediately he wondered if he should have said *Center*, the tattoo Emsley had got, instead of the man's real name.

Emsley shuffled forward, slightly facing away from Holbrook but peering at him sideways. "What're you looking at?" he demanded. "You know who I *am*?"

He wore black jeans and a black denim jacket, and he still looked twenty-five—the age he had been in 2003, when he had died in a car crash on the Hollywood Freeway.

"Have you," said Holbrook hesitantly, "been here—all this time?"

"I'll eat where I please! And take as long as I want! You wanna start some shit?"

"Center! *Dylan,* damn it! I'm Tom Holbrook, remember?"

Emsley was now holding a short knife. "How about I cut your face for you? You like that?"

Holbrook's chest went cold, and he was about to try conjuring a mirror when a mellow voice spoke from behind him. "You've got to wash dishes again, Dylan—you still don't have money for the check."

Emsley paused and frowned, and Holbrook glanced back toward their old table—and the figure now sitting on the far side of the pitcher of beer was John Atwater, lean and confident in a well-tailored suit and tie. "Here I am," Atwater said, "back of the bar in a solo game, right? Do you remember how to sit down?"

It occurred to Holbrook that he had not sat down since his death, and he was suddenly afraid that he would fall through the chair or something if he tried. He simply stood and stared at the man across the table, remotely aware of Emsley's footsteps receding into some other room.

Holbrook had been hunting Atwater for six years, in the real world and now in this flimsy makeshift post-mortem one, and he had at last come to the moment of confrontation—but the denunciations he had composed in a hundred sleepless nights had fled beyond his recall.

Instead he just burst out, "You killed her!"

Atwater smiled vaguely. "I don't remember things so well. Wait—the *APART* tattoo—I know who it is, you're a janitor—don't tell me—Calvert, Pete Calvert. Are you going to sit? Killed who?" He rocked his head to peer vaguely around at the room. "Dylan Emsley was just here."

"I'm *Tom Holbrook*, and you killed *Shasta*. I loved her, she was the most precious person on earth, but *you*, with no value at all, you took her away and killed her!"

"I'm sure you loved something, we all did. Yes, you're right, I *did* kill her, I do remember. With a gun. She disrespected me." He nodded. "One does what one has to do—I don't blame myself. I was always true to my own conscience." The last sentences had a rote sound, as if he'd said them many times.

"Your *conscience*? You were always true to your, your *narcissism*." Holbrook inhaled deeply. "*I* killed *myself* to get here, to find you. You're worth less than nothing, but I can at least make you into nothing." More loudly, he went on, "I'm going to make you cease to exist, do you understand that?"

He waited a few seconds for an answer, but Atwater just blinked at him; so Holbrook concentrated on his rage and frustration and thrust out his hand. And now he was holding a solid flat rectangle, and the back side of it was matte gray.

Atwater cocked his head, looking at the thing. "What have you got?"

"It's a mirror, damn you. Look into it."

"It's not a mirror. I remember what mirrors looked like."

Holbrook tilted the thing and looked down, but didn't see a reflection of the other side of the room; on the face of the rectangle was a picture of a man holding a baseball bat.

"That's a baseball card," explained Atwater. "They used to come with gum."

From another room came a shout from Emsley: "Soon as I'm done here I'm gonna kick your ass."

Atwater laughed softly. "You killed yourself? And then walked all the way down here—to find me? Downhill was easy, wasn't it? But you can't get back up again, it's too steep, go ahead and try it. Dylan figured that out before he got all the way down to the fringes. Stay with us—he likes you, I can tell. You can help him wash dishes for eternity."

Holbrook threw the rectangle at the floor—it disappeared before it hit the boards—and then took two running steps and lunged across the table, his clawed hands reaching for Atwater's throat.

But his hands struck gravel and he rolled across a pile of old headless Barbie dolls in suddenly cold air, under the gray sky. When he sat up, he was facing a rising cement slope; he looked over his shoulder and saw Atwater standing in the back doorway of Chasteen's.

"This is our place," Atwater said, "Center's and mine." For a moment he was gray-haired and fat, wearing a bathrobe, and then he was again the dark-haired man in the business suit. "I think you better go think up a place of your own."

"Fucker!" came Emsley's voice from inside.

Holbrook struggled to his feet, slipping on the dolls, and humiliation and despair helped him imagine a handgun in his right fist. A moment later he was gripping a soft, blurry object; he concentrated, and it hardened and focused into the shape of a big-caliber stainless-steel revolver.

He pointed it at Atwater and pulled the trigger, but there wasn't even a click as the hammer rose and fell. He pulled the trigger several more times, as Atwater looked on with raised eyebrows, and finally he thumbed the cylinder release and swung the cylinder out. All six chambers had jelly beans wedged in them, four of them with tiny firing pin dents.

Holbrook tossed the gun away, and didn't hear it strike anything. "The bell grows out!" he said loudly. His face was wet, and cold in the chilly breeze. "This will be the fringe soon! You'll fall off—" He kicked some dolls aside and straightened up, flexing his hands, and went on, "*I* won't be here—I know how to be reincarnated! You think I killed myself with no way back? Hah!" He pointed down at his sneakers. "See that shadow? I'm an over-easy, I died in contact with Hubcap Pete and he told me himself how to be born again back in the original world!"

He had flung that empty boast in sheer angry bravado, but Atwater reverted to the old man in the bathrobe again, and said, "Tom, tell me how!" His eyes were wide and his lower lip hung away from his teeth. "Tell me how and I'll tell you where Fall—*Sh-shasta*—is!"

Holbrook sighed deeply. "You're lying," he said unsteadily, "she's been dead six years, she wouldn't still—"

"How long do you think Emsley has been dead? Yes, the bell g-g-grows out, but you only have to shift uphill a bit from time to time, to stay even. She's in a…" He paused and smiled craftily, and he was dark-haired and wearing the suit again. "No, you tell me how, first."

Holbrook considered thinking up some arduous procedure to tell Atwater, but decided against giving the ghost any moments of hope at all.

"*Well…*" he said, "no. I can find her the same way I found you, and I'll tell *her* how.

She and I will do it together. We'll meet up again in the original world, while you stay here forever with Emsley."

And it may even be possible, he thought, hardly daring to let himself entertain the idea. Two of the ghosts here mentioned the possibility of reincarnation—maybe it's more than just a fantasy. *We can be a couple while you do it,* the woman in pink had said.

"We'll—we'll get a Ouija board," he went on, a bit shrilly, "and send you a wedding announcement!"

Atwater had stepped back, out of the gray light, his appearance flickering now between the trim executive and the fat old man. "I remember," he said quietly, "you always did hide behind that delusion." He closed the door, and Holbrook was alone with the scattered dolls in the sharply-tilted alley.

A sudden pain in the base of his spine let him know that he had sat down.

For some indeterminate time his mind was as empty as a fired shotgun shell. When thoughts began to occur, they were fragments: *That's it?...six years I've...impossible? even after...I gave up my life for...*

Then one thought was a complete sentence: *Shasta is here somewhere.*

He got to his feet. I can learn to make a real mirror, he told himself, and come back here then, but in the meantime, Shasta is here somewhere. I *must* be able to find her.

He walked along the alley in the direction he'd come from, and eventually came to what might have been the same street he had been following down from the square. He stepped in under the awning of a watch-repair shop and waited for a couple of mumbling pedestrians to pass, then took a deep breath and said, "Shasta DiMaio." And when the view of the street didn't shiver, he turned a few degrees to his right and said it again.

During the course of the next minute Holbrook shifted by short increments all the way around, saying her name over and over again, to the dark shop window and out to the street again, but there was no slightest ripple in his vision.

His chest had gone cold, and he was considering making his way back to the imaginary Chasteen's and asking Atwater to tell him where Shasta was, when a bitter thought occurred to him.

Facing out into the street, he made himself say, "Shasta Atwater," and at once his view of an abandoned gas station across the street was momentarily replaced by a glimpse of a building he knew he recognized. The yellow sign over the door and wide windows was obscured by spreading acacia branches, but the place was...Book City, a bookstore on Hollywood Boulevard that had closed in the 1990s. Holbrook couldn't recall ever having gone there with Shasta.

When his vision cleared, a thirty-foot long Chinese dragon was being paraded down the street, animated by a dozen running men inside its framework, and its bright orange catfish-whiskered face bobbed and swung as firecrackers popped on both sides of the street and threw shreds of red paper like rose petals—but before it had passed Holbrook, the painted fabric skin had evaporated, leaving only a line of men trudging downhill with long poles under their arms. Holbrook sprinted across the street after they had passed, and when he glanced back he saw that even the dozen men had disappeared.

"Shasta Atwater," he said dizzily, and again for a moment he saw the bookstore ahead of him.

He held onto a streetlight pole as he rounded the corner into a new street, but he didn't immediately let go of it and hurry onward.

Only two or three close buildings stood in this direction, because the street ended a dozen yards ahead in a tangle of cracked pavement and twisted rebar. Some hundreds of feet beyond the edge, Holbrook could see a diagonal cliff matching the slant of the street he was on, with a sawtooth pattern of low, ranch-style houses mounting up its sloped brink from left to right. One of the houses was missing the wall on this side, and he could just make out the intermittent blue glow of a TV set in one of the exposed rooms.

He walked carefully toward the broken-off end of this street, moving along the downhill-side curb, and when he got to within a couple of yards of the crumbled edge he clung to a stop-sign pole and peered across the gap.

A couple of telephone lines spanned the abyss from this street to a street on the other side, and several telephone poles dangled from the swinging lines. Holbrook concluded that the gap was the result of a piece of the bell having fallen away, for if the bell had simply split here, the power lines would have been stretched and snapped.

He inched closer and looked down; and though he expected it, he was disoriented to see that the far surface, exposed now in cross-section, was only a few hundred feet thick, with some crystalline regularities along the slanted bottom edge implying more structures on that side. Below it was just more gray sky.

Did she fall? he thought; and he shouted, "Shasta Atwater!" across the divide.

But the vision of the bookstore flashed for a moment in his sight, over there on the far side, and he sagged in relief; then he thought, *How am I to get there?*

The wind that blew up from the gulf was colder than the breeze in the streets behind him, and he turned, shivering, to retrace his steps—I can walk back up the slope of the bell to a point above the gap, he thought, no matter what Atwater said about the difficulty of it—when he heard a two-tone car horn, and, peering ahead, saw a bright green convertible stopped in the intersection, facing uphill. It looked like some late-1950s Cadillac, long and wide, with exaggeratedly tall tailfins.

He paused, expecting it to dissolve as the Chinese dragon had done, then realized that the driver must be Hubcap Pete himself.

Holbrook made his way as quickly as he could along the tilted street back to the intersection. The car horn honked again, and Holbrook could see the driver clearly now—it was a white-haired man with a bushy moustache, in a Hawaiian shirt, and he was waving one tanned arm.

"Apart!" the man yelled. "Quit clowning around and get over here."

Holbrook heard another car approaching, and looked up the street. The white Dodge Dart he had seen earlier, its engine running at last, was barreling down toward the green convertible; it swerved around it, its tires squealing, and went bobbing away downhill.

Holbrook saw no other traffic, and he hurried across the incline to the driver's side of the convertible; and when the driver waved impatiently at the passenger side, he scrambled around to that side and got in and closed the door.

"You're—Hubcap Pete," Holbrook said as the engine roared and he was pressed back into the seat by sudden acceleration uphill.

"Right," the man said. "You didn't hang around at the square. Didn't that Martinez fellow in the desert tell you to?" The car slanted to the right onto a freeway onramp that Holbrook had not noticed on his walk down the street.

"No." Holbrook spoke loudly over the fluttering headwind. "Anyway, I was looking for a guy."

"Martinez said you have something important to tell me. What is it?"

Holbrook had forgotten that Martinez had said that. "Uh," he said helplessly, "don't jump. This place will collapse if you do."

"Huh. That was it? Well, don't worry, this place won't collapse if I have anything to say about it."

The freeway rose above the surrounding buildings, and when Holbrook shifted around in the seat to glance back, he saw a figure swinging from one of the abyss-spanning telephone lines; from this distance he couldn't be sure, but it seemed to be a heavy-set man with a bathrobe flapping around his bare legs. Holbrook's chest suddenly felt empty.

"Damn, I think—" he began.

"Yeah, that's your guy," said Hubcap Pete, nodding without glancing away from the lanes ahead, "crossing to the other side. You got the plumb bob?"

"Can you get over there?" Holbrook asked anxiously, still bracing himself on his left arm to stare back at the distant dangling figure. "He's going to kill her again!" He squinted at the sections of the edge that he could see. "Is there a bridge you could take?"

"That gap just happened a day or so ago. Bridges don't grow that fast." Hubcap Pete took one hand from the wheel and pointed at the dashboard. "The air-conditioner control knob."

Holbrook noticed that the knob was missing. "So? No, I don't have it. Can you—"

"We'll loop around the inside edge of the gap. Probably be there before he is, even if he doesn't fall. And he can't kill anybody, they're all dead already. Didn't that woman in the booth give it to you, up by the square, right after you landed?"

"Well, hurry. What, the goddamn control knob of your air-conditioner? No, nobody—" Holbrook paused. "Oh. Yeah, it had a string wrapped around the post. She said it was a yo-yo."

The freeway curved to the right, and Pete steered into the right lane and stayed on it when it split away and became an offramp; a red traffic light hung over the cross street ahead, and Pete slowed to a stop. Lush oleander bushes screened the view to the sides. Holbrook was breathing fast, and he thought this area of Purgatory smelled like a newly-opened jar of vitamin pills.

"She didn't know what it was," Pete said. "You're supposed to use it as a plumb bob." He glanced around the interior of the car and sighed. "I'll make you another." Before

Holbrook could ask why, Pete went on, "What did that Martinez guy tell you about me? I've dealt with him before."

"He said that you died while you were in Ouija contact with somebody…here," Holbrook said, waving around at the street and the bushes. He rubbed his left arm, which had gone to sleep from being braced on the back of the seat.

"Somebody here." Pete nodded, staring at the red traffic light. "Yes, it was a man I had killed. I was trying to…apologize?" He laughed shortly. "Explain, excuse myself? But his wife, his widow I should say, had not gone to bed after all, and heard me speaking to him at the Ouija board, and she realized it was me who had killed him. She fetched a gun and shot me in the back." He squinted sideways at Holbrook. "Martinez wants you to find out about me, doesn't he, and then report back?"

After a pause in which the light turned green, Holbrook nodded.

Pete made a left turn onto a broad street between old wooden tenements that rapidly and noisily extruded balconies and then retracted them. Shingles and scraps of lumber whirled away in the wind. "Did he tell you why he wants to know about me? My real name, the names of my family, friends, the woman who killed me? Most of them are probably still alive in the original world—I haven't seen any of them come through here, anyway. No? He wants *leverage* on me."

Holbrook tried to lift his hand in an *and?* gesture, but his arm was still numb.

Pete went on, "He wants to get me to interrogate new arrivals, to learn their poor little secrets—Social Security numbers and bank passwords so he can empty accounts before survivors even know a person's dead, learn where stuff's hidden, maybe get insider trading tips, get medical and legal details for possible blackmail…spirits here are so dumb that they'd tell me all those things, but I won't do it." He looked away from the street to give Holbrook a piercing glance. "Would you?"

"No." Holbrook thought about it. "I don't know. It'd depend on whether he could get me something I badly want, I guess, from his side." Holbrook mentally reviewed the agreement he'd made with Martinez, which looked impossible to keep since Hubcap Pete knew what it was. "Wouldn't you like revenge on the woman who killed you?"

Pete grimaced. "Hell no. It was redundant when she shot me—I killed myself, everything that was worthwhile in myself, when I killed her husband. I think I've finally figured that out, in my time here. That's the value of this halfway house, it gives spirits a little while to get straightened out, to reconsider stuff." He glanced at Holbrook, who was craning his neck to try to see over the rooftops, and added, "We're getting there, we're getting there."

Holbrook slouched back down in his seat, massaging his arm, and he thought about the spirits he had met here. "*Do* they ever reconsider? They don't seem very bright, mostly."

"Some do. That fellow in the Dodge Dart that drove past me back there, I think he's finally ready to make what frail amends he can to his daughter. I hope he catches up to her before she flies off the rim—she's pretty quick on that skateboard."

Holbrook recalled the little girl talking about the man who'd been trying to get the Dodge started, and he remembered catching a momentary peripheral glimpse of her as a taller person. "She said that when you fly off the bottom edge of the bell you find out what grade you're in. And one guy seemed to think you wind up in a courtroom. Martinez called it definition."

"It's not a bell," said Pete irritably as he passed a slow-moving horse trailer with half a dozen identical children's faces at the barred windows. "Purgatory's a flat disk, spinning. It's centrifugal force, not gravity, that makes it seem as if the outer sections are tilted down. And as the edges break away, new buildings grow up out of the central square's pavement, and move outward."

Holbrook thought of the miniature building he had seen sticking up out of a fissure between the bricks in the square. And I caved in one wall of it, he thought, trying to pull it out. Don't mention that now.

"So what does happen," he asked, "when you fly off the edge?"

"Well, I haven't done it *yet*," said Pete, "but I get the idea there's a *real* primary out there, with something you could say was like actual gravity. Like a solar system, and every spirit finds its proper orbit, depending on what it consists of, around something that radiates and reciprocates…good stuff. Joy, you know? Contentment. Intelligence. Communication. The ones in the closer orbits get brighter, but the ones in the remote, colder orbits shrink down to hardly anything." He shrugged. "Yeah, I guess it's like definition, or getting assigned to a class level, or a verdict in a courtroom. But really it's more like plain physics."

And pleading *nolo contendere* probably wouldn't get you any second chance, thought Holbrook. Even if it *did* spell reincarnation backward.

Hubcap Pete had steered onto another freeway onramp, and within a hundred yards it had risen high above the surrounding streets and buildings. Looking over Pete's shoulder, beyond the rushing rail Holbrook could see the wedge of gray-sky emptiness that cleaved the cityscape below, though from this distance he couldn't hope to see a figure clinging to a telephone line that stretched from one edge of the gap to the other.

"A couple of these, these spirits," he said hesitantly, "mentioned the possibility of reincarnation. Is that…something that can happen?"

"Yeah," said Pete, apparently angry, "it can, for distinct over-easy spirits like you and me. You want to know how?" Without waiting for an answer, he went on, "I'll tell you. You find a spirit here who's in Ouija contact with someone in the original world—they'll be holding telephones or wearing headphones or something, and have their eyes closed, is how you can tell, and they'll be moving something back and forth, like with shuffleboard or croquet, or they'll be working a Rubik's cube with letters on the squares. What they're really moving is the sliding gadget on a Ouija board over in the original world. And you snatch their headphones and put them on yourself, and grab the Rubik's Cube or whatever, so now it's *you* that the poor sap back in the original world is in contact with."

Playing shuffleboard or croquet, thought Holbrook—or jigging a motorized wheelchair back and forth.

He spread the fingers of his right hand. "So?"

"Your other hand is numb, isn't it?" said Pete. "I know how that is. You've heard of amputees who feel itchy and cold in the missing limb? They call that a phantom limb. Same thing here—except that you're a whole phantom body. And *you'd* like to be reincarnated into a *real* one again. Shit."

"What, you take over the body of the, the *poor sap* in the original world, bump his soul out? Martinez said that could happen. But that's not really—"

"That's *dybbuks*," interrupted Pete, "and it doesn't work very well. I've seen 'em come right back here after a little while. No, when you're in Ouija contact with somebody in the original world, you can see all the souls near him—it looks like a big dark plain, and the souls show up as sparks. For real reincarnation, you look for two that are overlapping, and you take the smaller, weaker one—bump it aside and step in."

"The smaller one…" began Holbrook.

"Forget about it. It's not something you'd do, or I'm wrong about you."

"Wrong about me? You don't know anything about me at all."

"I know you're here to figure out whether to blame a girl or not. Same as me."

"You've got it wrong. I'm here to—"

"I know, I know, delete a guy. Tell me another, phantom boy."

Holbrook opened his mouth to reply angrily, but remembered that Pete was apparently taking him to where Shasta was; and he had noticed the oval passenger-side mirror, which was attached only by a clamp to the door he had his elbow on. He sat back, resolved to bide his time.

From up here on the freeway bridge, he could just see the central square and the fountain off to his right, and beyond them more streets radiating outward. In the middle distance another freeway bridge arched above the domes and chimneys. It was clear that Purgatory was indeed flat—he could dimly make out the irregular far edge, miles away.

"If we didn't have to get *your* business settled," growled Pete, "I'd right now be driving over all the freeways and main streets, always counterclockwise, to keep it all spinning; this car has mass, inertia, traction. If I don't go around and look at it all, it gets blurry, and if the spinning slows down, pieces fall off. Like they been doing! That's why you need a plumb bob." He shook his head. "God knows what's become of the one I left for you in the square—I'll have to make you another."

As the freeway bridge began to descend, Holbrook caught a last glimpse of the gap to the left, and he saw that they were now on the other side of it; and the car's turn signal indicator began clacking as Pete slowed the car and drifted it into the right lane.

He took the next offramp, a narrow gravel-paved path, and the car slewed almost broadside-on before Pete wrestled it back in line. At the end of the track was a cement-paved road with deep diagonal tining grooves.

As Pete steered the car left, across the grooves, he said, "Your girl's down this way. You should try that exit in the rain."

Holbrook peered through the windshield at the crowded barns and windmills alongside the lanes in front of them. "It rains here?"

"You think those clouds are just for show? Shit. You want to see some real rain?"

"Just get us to the bookstore," said Holbrook shortly, staring out to the side now at a fenced field dotted with rusted iron statues of dogs. He hoped any rain here was no more substantial than the roofs.

"Sure," said Pete, "never mind if half of Purgatory turns to mush or falls off." He lifted one finger from the steering wheel to point ahead. "Her bookstore place is coming up on the right. Hop out—I'll catch you again, after."

With luck there won't be any after, thought Holbrook; Shasta and I can live forever in the bookstore, as Atwater and Emsley appear to be doing at Chasteen's. As long as Purgatory doesn't collapse!

But, "Okay," he said as the car rocked to a halt and he saw the yellow Book City sign over the long windows. "Now get back on your usual route," he added anxiously as he got out and closed the door.

Just as the car started to move forward and speed up, Holbrook grabbed the passenger-side door mirror with both hands; he was yanked off his feet, but as he rolled to a stop on the gravel road, his bleeding hands still clutched the mirror, and the green car was accelerating away. A church steeple and a water tower bowed perceptibly as the car passed between them.

Holbrook sat up, wincing, and then painfully got to his feet. He was reassured by each ache and twinge, though, for they were sensations that real bodies had—Hubcap Pete's remark about a *phantom body* had scared him.

When he turned toward the bookstore, the front door was open and Shasta herself was actually there, standing on the threshold no more than ten feet away. She was wearing a blue denim jacket and skirt, and she was the youthful college student he had recited the Housman lines to at their last night in Chasteen's, not the tired woman who had kissed him after the dinner at Mastro's in 2006.

For several seconds Holbrook simply stared at her.

At last, "I don't want that," she said, and it shook him to hear her well-remembered voice again.

"No, you don't," Holbrook said quickly. "It's poison, don't even look at it. Shasta, it's me, it's Tom Holbrook!" He looked back, in the direction of the long gap in Purgatory's fabric, but he didn't see a tall man in a business suit or a fat old man in a bathrobe.

"This thing," he went on, bending down to slap the cone-shaped back of the mirror, "is to protect you from—" He shook his head. "Can I come in?"

"Tom Holbrook," she said. "Yes, that was your original name, wasn't it? I remember you. You were one of the ones who got a tattoo." With her free hand she pulled the right side of the jacket away, and he could see the FALL tattoo partly covered by the strap of a white tank-top. "That's my handle."

Holbrook glanced down at his own shoulder; his T-shirt had dried out and didn't cling now, and he tugged it down to expose his own tattoo.

"Apart," said Shasta. "That's right. I married…Things, didn't I."

"Don't think about that now." Holbrook bent to pick up the mirror, then crouched to grip it with both abraded hands. "Heavier than it looks," he said, lifting it. "Let me just get this inside."

Shasta stepped aside, glancing at the streamlined mirror housing Holbrook carried.

"That'll probably make the shop move downhill faster," she said.

"Oh!" Holbrook paused. "I'll leave it outside."

"No, bring it in. Who do you want to poison? Whatever's in that thing might make somebody sick, but nobody dies here."

"Well…John. Things. And this is a mirror."

"A mirror. And you want to break it, after he looks into it, *steps* into it." She pushed back her dark hair and looked directly at Holbrook. "Why?"

"Do you, uh, remember how you died?"

"Yes, he shot me. Is that why you want to erase him? That's between him and me."

Holbrook had shuffled in through the door, and he set the mirror cone-up, facedown on the counter by the cash register. Tall close-set bookshelves made narrow corridors of the building's interior, and in one corner by the window stood a dusty piano with boxes stacked on it.

He turned around to face Shasta. "Do *you* want to show him the mirror?—and then break it?"

She smiled in evident bafflement. “No.”

Holbrook stared at her for a moment. “I trust you won’t object when I do it,” he said, in a tone that came out more defiant than he had intended.

She shrugged and leaned back against a wall of bookshelves, and Holbrook noticed that none of the spines had titles. “Apart,” she said, “there’s something you should know about me.”

“What’s that?”

“I don’t know, but you should know it.”

The wall behind her flickered as gold-stamped titles now appeared on all the book spines; it seemed to be the same title on all of them, but Holbrook was standing too far away to read it.

“We can stay here,” he said. “You and I, forever. If Things comes, I’ll break him in the mirror.”

Shasta blinked around at the shelves, humming to herself, and jumped slightly when her eyes fell on him. “I’m sorry, what was it?”

“I said I’ll break him in the mirror. Things, John Atwater, your one-time husband.” She was still staring at him blankly, so he added, "I'm Tom Holbrook, remember?"

She reached toward him, and he saw that her hand touched his arm, though he didn't feel it. "Wait," she said, "I remember, if I concentrate." She nodded several times and then looked at him with evident recognition. "Apart," she said; "Tom—you're dead now. You don't need me, you don't need the excuse of me anymore, there's no one to hide away from anymore."

To his surprise, he was suddenly angry. "I'm not hiding from him! I got this mirror to kill him! I'm ready—"

"Not from him. You never got married, did you? You were never that close to anybody."

"I wanted to marry *you*—you know that!—but you married *him*, and he *killed* you."

She smiled. "And after that? You never found somebody, even then? It's been a long time."

"Nobody could replace *you*—and then I couldn't think of anything but finding him and killing him, for what he did."

"Yes. Even after I was dead, I was still your excuse." She stepped away from the wall, and before turning to face her again he peered at the shelves. The title on all the books was *The House At Pooh Corner*, though as he watched, it changed to *Los Angeles Extended Area Telephone Directory*.

"Don't snoop," she said from behind him.

When he turned around, she was buttoning up her jacket. She gave him an empty look, and he wasn't sure she still recognized him. "I don't know if this has done you or me any good," she said, "but I believe I'm finally tired of recasting this place uphill."

Holbrook raised one spread hand in mute inquiry.

"I suggest we stroll down by the terraces," she said, stepping toward the door.

"Down's not a good idea," Holbrook began, lifting the mirror from the counter, but a cry from across the street made him spin in that direction.

For a moment it was a shabby old man in a bathrobe and bedroom slippers who was stepping out from between two cartoon outhouses; and then it was John Atwater in his suit, and the outhouses flickered behind him with a glimpse of Chasteen's.

"Apart!" Atwater called again.

Holbrook stepped out onto the street, hefting his mirror. "Right here." The cold wind was from downhill, carrying the scent of wet stone.

Atwater was staring at the gravel below his polished shoes, and he took two more steps and then halted. "You found her," he said, and his voice was pitched higher than before, "Just as I said. Now come through with your part of the bargain."

"Things!" exclaimed Shasta; Atwater didn't reply to that, though her voice shook him into a few seconds of bathrobe-clad decrepitude.

Then, restored to his suit and tie and dark hair but still staring at his shoes, Atwater said, "Does he really know Hubcap Pete?"

"Does who?" asked Shasta. "Oh, this guy? Yes, Pete drove him here, in his big green car. He said, *I'll catch you later.* Oh! And it's Apart, you remember, with the tattoo?"

"Look at me!" called Holbrook, raising the mirror.

Atwater glanced up, then quickly lowered his eyes again. "So you've got a real mirror now! But you owe me—*tell me how to do it!* You two can do it together, like you said, but you promised to tell *me* how."

Shasta glanced at Holbrook. "He never did know how to do it," she said. "But *I'm* going to the terraces."

"I mean *reincarnation*," shouted Atwater, wavering like a body viewed under agitated water. "He knows how to be born again in the original world." When his appearance came back into focus, he tipped a quick glance at Holbrook. "You *do* know how, don't you?"

"It—doesn't matter to you," said Holbrook, turning away from him to face Shasta.

She rocked her head downhill and raised her eyebrows.

He looked uphill, at the road ascending between silos and lines of barbed wire fence, then sighed and stepped downhill beside her. The mirror seemed to be getting heavier.

Logs had been half-buried crosswise in the road, and the two of them stepped carefully from one to another for a hundred sloping feet, and then there was level flagstone pavement, with an ornate iron railing on the downhill side and stairs to right and left. A few figures were visible on the stairs, all shuffling downward. The gray light was dimmer now—the overcast sky was lower, and closer in front of them, and marbled with black. The wind from below was damp.

"Tut-tut," said Shasta as she guided them down the stairs on the right, past an old man struggling to get a walker down the steps, "it looks like rain."

The tall buildings on either side looked abandoned—row upon row of glassless windows in streaked cement cliffs, tangles of fallen lumber and cables between close walls, unmoored satellite dishes swinging like windchimes. After Holbrook and Shasta had descended several levels, the railings on the downhill side of the landings were weathered railway ties bolted together.

At one point Holbrook glanced back up the way they'd come, and saw Atwater's round head peering down over the wooden beam one flight above them, his scanty gray hair fluttering.

Shasta had seen him too. "Like old times," she said, "except in those days I'd be walking with him, and it'd be you who was following."

Holbrook shifted the ever-heavier mirror to a more comfortable position, and didn't answer. He promised himself that he would soon ask her, plead with her, to turn back; but he was afraid that she would insist on going on alone, if he did.

Their way grew steeper, and instead of a slope of terraces connected by stairways, they were now descending something like a broad concrete fire escape. They paused to rest on one of the decks, stepping to the rail to get out of the way as half a dozen men in business suits trotted past them, following one of their number who carried a small flag.

Holbrook took hold of the rail with his free hand and looked down, and he saw that the wall widened out in a roofed gallery a flight or two below, but beyond that there was nothing but churning clouds—and he remembered his view of the broken-away gap with the telephone lines stretching across it.

And he recalled what Hubcap Pete had told him: *Purgatory's a flat disk, spinning. It's centrifugal force, not gravity, that makes it seem as if the outer sections are tilted down.*

We must be perpendicular to the souls in the central square, he thought. Still gripping the rail, he leaned out, now squinting straight up—the wall extended vertically as far as he could see, and in the misty distance up there it did seem to bristle with what must be rooftops and towers.

If the Empire State Building were ever to grow in the square, he thought, from here I'd see it sticking out horizontally.

"For God's sake," he said finally, crouching to set the mirror at his feet, and then massaging his arm, "let's go back up while we still can." Even without the burden of the mirror, his phantom thigh muscles ached as he forced himself to stand up straight against the increased gravity.

Shasta turned to him with a concerned look. "But Tom, we *can't*. You can't—even if you leave that mirror behind here. Nobody ever makes it back up, from this far down. Didn't you know that?" Holbrook heard labored shuffling on the next floor above them, and Shasta waved up toward it. "Yes, that's Things. *He* knows it—he only followed us because he believes you *will* tell him the reincarnation secret. I don't think he could *do* it—I don't think he'd stretch that far, as he is—but you're right not to tell him about it."

Spots of chill touched Holbrook's hands and face, and he stepped back under the deck overhead as raindrops splashed on the rail and began to darken the floor on that side.

"And rain makes the fringe heavier," Shasta added.

Holbrook was breathing fast, from panic as much as from cumulative fatigue. "Stretch?" he said. "Do *you* know how to do it? How to—be reborn in the original world?"

She nodded. "I've been here long enough, and sometimes I've listened and remembered—though *I* couldn't reach, either."

"Listen," Holbrook said, "I have a shadow. You can't see it now, but maybe you noticed it when everywhere wasn't so tilted and dark. I think you *could* reach, if you did it *with* me." He waved in the direction the trooping businessmen had taken, and lowered his voice. "People come down here—surely one of them will have headphones on, be in Ouija contact with the someone in the original world, eventually. If we just wait here."

"Here won't be here for long, I think." Shasta laughed softly. "And you'd kill a child—two children, real ones!—to get us lives again? You always did strike *poses*, Tom."

It looks like a big dark plain, Hubcap Pete had said, *and the souls show up as sparks. For real reincarnation, you look for two that are overlapping, and you take the smaller one.*

"Oh," Holbrook said. "Oh." He sat down beside the mirror. "Weaker and inexperienced, sure—it's the soul of a child that hasn't been born yet, that you bump aside. Take the place of."

"Yes. You hadn't guessed that part of it?"

"I hadn't thought about it." He shrugged hopelessly. "Pete said I wouldn't do it."

"What if I told you that one of those tourists who marched past us just now was wearing headphones?"

Holbrook peered down the long cement floor in the direction those men had taken. They had either gone up or down the stairs that lay at that end, but he would certainly be able to follow the rhythmic drumming of their footsteps either way.

And then what? Snatch the headphones and put them on, scan the sparks on that dark plain and reach out for one of them? To steal a second life for myself by eliminating an innocent one?

He sighed and shook his head.

"I made it up," said Shasta, starting toward the stairs. "None of them had headphones."

Holbrook got wearily to his feet, hefting the mirror, which now weighed as much as a bowling ball. "They weren't moving right anyway, now that I think of it. Pete said that people in contact kind of jiggle back and forth."

He followed her to the stairs, and as he struggled down the steps after her, he saw that the stairs ended at the foot of this flight. They had reached the bottom, or outermost, level.

This was the wider area, the long roofed gallery that he had seen from the deck above, and as he stepped out of the stairwell he saw that it was a two-lane street, with a railing over on the abyss-facing side. Shasta hurried across the lanes and peered down over this last railing. Within moments her hair was pasted flat by the strengthening rain.

"Infinity," she called back to Holbrook, who had put down the mirror and was leaning against the inside wall. She waved at the cloudy emptiness beyond the rail. "Out there you find your level of buoyancy—inward, in the sunlight, or out in the cold dark." She peered down to the right, then pointed. "Look!"

The rain was gusting all the way to the inside wall now, and Holbrook pushed away from it and walked carefully across the glistening pavement to stand beside her at the rail. She was squinting through strands of dark wet hair, and he looked in the direction she was pointing.

The edge was uneven, and a hundred yards below them to the right a long section of masonry extended downward for several more levels—but it was swaying in the rain. Holbrook could see white faces and waving arms.

Then it separated from the Purgatory disk, and, along with a lot of chunks of tumbling cement, it spun away into the clouds. The whole edge shook, and Holbrook clung uselessly to the railing.

He was about to insist that they climb back up at least a couple of levels, when a hoarse shout from behind made him turn around.

John Atwater had fallen down the last few steps from the level above, and he was rolling on the wet cement in front of the stairwell, tangled in his bathrobe.

"Shasta!" he yelled, "make him take me with you! You both still owe me that much!"

"I've got what I owe you right here," said Holbrook, hurrying back across the street to where he had left the mirror.

Shasta turned to face both of them. "We're not doing the reincarnation," she called to Atwater. "And it's far to late to try to get back up." As if to emphasize her words, the pavement and walls shivered, and Shasta flailed her arms and then took two fast steps toward the wall as the railing fell away behind her. "We're all about to find our levels of buoyancy."

Get our verdicts, thought Holbrook, learn what grade we're assigned to, find the orbits our quotients of joy naturally fall into.

The roaring of a car engine was echoing now along the roofed roadway.

"Fine," said Atwater, perhaps sobbing, "but tell *me* how."

Holbrook was standing only a few yards to Atwater's right. "You couldn't do it," Holbrook told him, bending to once again lift the ponderous mirror in both hands, "and I won't tell you how anyway. But you can look into this."

"Shasta," said Atwater, crouching forward away from the wall, into the slanting rain, "*you'll* tell me. You love me."

"I'm sure I did love you," replied Shasta, with no animosity.

As you never managed to love me, thought Holbrook. Who wouldn't have *killed* you.

"But Tom's right," Shasta went on, "you couldn't do it. And I won't tell you either. You'd only hurt yourself if you tried."

Atwater's broad head, streaked now with wet gray hair, swiveled from her to Holbrook. "After everything," he said, more quietly, "you both betray me. You're both responsible—you *know* you're both responsible!—for the place in which I'd find *myself* on that...that judgmental periodic table!" He waved out toward the void. "The quickest to decay, in the remotest orbit, on the ocean floor with no buoyancy at all! Beyond the reach of any light, intelligence, wit! *Forever!*"

Atwater turned to face Holbrook, and he stood up straight, and for just a moment he was again the dark-haired man in the business suit. "Very well," he said. "Hold up your mirror."

Holbrook stared at him for several seconds, then spun around and hurled the mirror out at the space where the railing had been. He had thrown it as hard as he could, but it just cleared the edge.

"Work out your own damnation," he said breathlessly, "in fear and trembling."

The sound of a car engine had grown louder, and now headlight beams gleamed on their three wet faces and illuminated the slanting raindrops, and the big green convertible came nosing down the wall-side lane from the direction where the section of Purgatory had broken away.

The squeal of brakes echoed up and down the enclosed street, and Hubcap Pete levered open the driver's side door and climbed out onto the puddled pavement. His moustache drooped and his Hawaiian shirt was clinging to him. He held out one hand with something dangling from it.

Holbrook pushed wet hair back from his forehead and squinted, and saw that it was a car's window crank swinging on a foot-long piece of string.

"A replacement plumb bob," said Pete, speaking loudly over the drumming of the rain. "Now you can't use the air conditioning *or* roll the window up. Don't lose this one."

Atwater shambled up to stand beside the front bumper, wrapping his sodden bathrobe around himself. "I'll give you a thousand dollars," he said distinctly, "to drive me up out of here."

"Talk to the new owner," Pete said, nodding toward Holbrook. "I've driven enough miles by now to know where I am. This boy's got a sense of direction, but he has some miles to go before he parks."

Atwater scrambled forward, but wound up sitting down heavily after Pete shoved him back with the palm of one hand.

Holbrook took hold of the string the window crank dangled from. "What do I do with it?"

"You hold it up," said Pete impatiently, "and see if the buildings are still vertical, still parallel with the string! If they seem to be tilted more than the string is, toward the central square, then you gotta drive around more, faster, to speed up the disk so it doesn't collapse. And *look* at everything, to keep it all distinct! These people deserve whatever time they care to take, here, to reconsider, if they can. Or maybe they don't deserve it—but I like to give it to 'em anyway."

He walked around the hood of the car and crossed the other lane to stand beside Shasta, near the gap where the railing had been. Atwater still sat where he had fallen beside the inner wall, staring emptily at Holbrook.

Holbrook looked away from him, and met Shasta's gaze.

He raised his eyebrows and waved toward the passenger side, but she smiled and shook her head.

"Honestly," she said, perhaps in emphasis, perhaps as a parting piece of advice.

He nodded, acknowledging this final refusal. "That's okay," he said; then, "Really, it's okay."

"Go," said Pete, "this section of the disk is going to fall off any minute. Straight ahead, and take the next ramp on your left, that'll get you back up onto the freeway. And drive careful—the right side mirror is gone."

Holbrook slowly climbed into the driver's seat and pulled the door closed. The dashboard glowed green in the dimness, and he saw that a big keypad was mounted above the radio, facing the driver.

The gear-shift lever was up in the Park position, and he tentatively gunned the engine; echoes rang away along the wet lanes.

"Will you *go?*" said Pete.

Holbrook pulled the lever down into Drive, and the car moved forward. He pressed the accelerator and the car sped up, and when he saw the ramp approaching on the left, he looked into the rear-view mirror. Atwater was still sitting on the pavement back there, and Hubcap Pete and Shasta were standing by the gap.

Shasta waved, and after a moment he sighed and lifted his right hand from the wheel and held it up, fingers spread in the rain; then he gripped the wheel with both hands and steered into the ramp.

It was steep and narrow, and he drove slowly, peering ahead at the curving walls; and he jumped when the glow of the headlights in the tight passage was dimmed by gray light from behind—when he glanced into the rear-view mirror, he saw that this curl of the ramp was now the lowest part of the Purgatory fringe, and the abyss yawned only a few yards in back of his rear wheels. He sped up, making the tires squeal around the turns.

The headlights again provided the only light after he had followed the spiral ramp a dozen yards farther, and then the cement walls were lit from ahead. The ramp straightened out and soon curved to the right, and he saw that he was on a freeway onramp under the eternal gray sky, with office buildings or warehouses on either side. A few indistinct cars moved along the lanes, and he signaled for a turn and merged into the left lane.

I'm moving clockwise, he thought. I'll have to find an interchange and get going the other way.

The radio popped and buzzed, and then a voice from the speaker said, "Pete? Come over here. Have you met up with Apart yet? Tom Holbrook? Pete, are you there?"

Holbrook unclenched his right hand from the steering wheel and reached for the keypad. One letter at a time, pausing frequently to look at the ghostly traffic ahead and ignoring the momentary glimpse of the dark plain, he typed in, NO AND I DONT THINK I EVER WILL JACK AND JILL HAVE GONE DOWN THE HILL.

He switched off the radio.